lit
Miss
Bossy
by Roger Hargreaves

On Monday Little Miss Bossy went for a walk.

She met Mr Nosey.

"Where are you going?" he asked.

"Mind your own business," she retorted.

On Tuesday she met Mr Noisy.

He was singing.

Noisily, of course.

"Shut up!" she told him.

On Wednesday she met Mr Happy.

He was smiling.

As usual.

"Take that silly smile off your face!" she said.

As you can imagine, Little Miss Bossy wasn't very popular.

To say the least.

Now, little did Miss Bossy realise, but somebody had seen her bossing Mr Nosey about.

And that same somebody had seen her bossing Mr Noisy about.

And that self-same somebody had seen her bossing Mr Happy about.

The wizard (whose name incidentally was Wilfred) went home, thinking.

"Something really ought to be done about Miss Bossy," he thought to himself as he walked along.

When he arrived home he went straight to his library and took down a large red book from a bookshelf.

It was rather dusty as it hadn't been read for some time.

"Let's see now," he said to himself as he settled into an armchair.

He turned to page three hundred and four.

At the top of the page it said:

'HOW TO STOP PEOPLE BEING BOSSY'.

Wilfred the Wizard read the page very carefully, shut the book, put it back on the bookshelf, and grinned.

A particularly wizardy sort of a grin.

The day after, which was Thursday, Little Miss Bossy met somebody who was fast asleep.

As usual.

Mr Lazy.

"Wake up!" she said bossily, and prodded him in the tummy.

"Ouch!" protested Mr Lazy.

But.

Behind Miss Bossy, Wilfred the Wizard, who had been following her, said something too.

Under his breath.

A wizardy word he'd learned from page three hundred and four.

And, do you know what happened?

Suddenly, as if by magic, which is true, there appeared on Miss Bossy's feet a pair of boots.

One minute they weren't there.

The next minute they were.

Miss Bossy looked down in alarm.

They were magic boots and, being magic boots, they could speak to each other.

"Hello Left," said the right boot.

"Hello Right," said the left boot.

"Ready when you are," said Right.

"Right," said Left.

And off they set.

Left. Right, Left. Right. Left. Right. Left. Right.

Faster and faster.

Marching poor Little Miss Bossy along.

Little Miss Bossy couldn't do a thing about it.

Mr Lazy was much amused.

"Well done Wilfred," he chuckled.

Wilfred winked a wizardy wink.

Those boots marched Little Miss Bossy for five miles.

She was exhausted.

"Ready Left," said the right boot.

"Ready," replied Left.

"Atten..." said Right.

"...shun!" said Left.

And they came to a halt.

Little Miss Bossy was quite out of breath.

She tried to take off her boots.

But it was impossible.

Along came Wilfred.

"Those," said Wilfred, pointing to the boots, "are only for people who are too bossy!"

"Make them go away AT ONCE!" cried Miss Bossy, stamping her foot.

Well, at least she tried to stamp her foot, but the boot wouldn't.

"We're out of stamps," chuckled Right.

Left giggled.

"YOU...WILL...DO...AS...I...SAY!!" shouted Miss Bossy.

"Ready when you are," said Right.

"Right away," replied Left.

"Quick march!"

And off they set again.

Left.

Right.

Left.

Right.

Left.

Right.

For ten miles.

And then they stopped again.

And along came Wilfred.

"MAKE THESE STUPID BOOTS GO AWAY,"
shouted Miss Bossy.

"Only if you say the magic word," replied Wilfred.

Miss Bossy thought.

And thought.

And thought again.

"Please," she said.

"That's better," smiled Wilfred.

And he said the wizardy word again, under his breath, from page three hundred and four.

The boots disappeared, as if by magic!

"Now then," said Wilfred sternly, wagging his finger. "Stop being bossy, or you know what will happen."

Miss Bossy nodded.

Miserably.

"Very well," smiled Wilfred.

And went.

And do you know something?

From then on, until now off, Little Miss Bossy was a changed person.

Not bossy at all.

And you know why, don't you?

You know what she's afraid of?

Bossyboots!!

# Fantastic offers for Little Miss fans!

**Collect all your Mr. Men or Little Miss books in these superb durable collectors' cases!**
Only £5.99 inc. postage and packing, these wipe-clean, hard-wearing cases will give all your Mr. Men or Little Miss books a beautiful new home!

**Keep track of your collection with this giant-sized double-sided Mr. Men and Little Miss Collectors' poster.**
Collect 6 tokens and we will send you a brilliant giant-sized double-sided collectors' poster! Simply tape a £1 coin to cover postage and packaging in the space provided and fill out the form overleaf.

**STICK £1 COIN HERE** (for poster only)

cut along the dotted line and return this whole page

**Only need a few Little Miss or Mr. Men to complete your set?** You can order any of the titles on the back of the books from our Mr. Men order line on 0870 787 1724. Orders should be delivered between 5 and 7 working days.

**TO BE COMPLETED BY AN ADULT**

To apply for any of these great offers, ask an adult to complete the details below and send this whole page with the appropriate payment and tokens, to: MR. MEN CLASSIC OFFER, PO BOX 715, HORSHAM RH12 5WG

☐ Please send me a giant-sized double-sided collectors' poster.

AND ☐ I enclose 6 tokens and have taped a £1 coin to the other side of this page.

☐ Please send me ☐ Mr. Men Library case(s) and/or ☐ Little Miss library case(s) at £5.99 each inc P&P

☐ I enclose a cheque/postal order payable to Egmont UK Limited for £..........

OR ☐ Please debit my MasterCard / Visa / Maestro / Delta account (delete as appropriate) for £..........

Card no. ☐☐☐☐☐☐☐☐☐☐☐☐☐☐☐☐☐☐☐ Security code ☐☐☐

Issue no. (if available) ☐ Start Date ☐☐/☐☐/☐☐ Expiry Date ☐☐/☐☐/☐☐

Fan's name: .......... Date of birth: ..........

Address: ..........

..........

.......... Postcode: ..........

Name of parent / guardian: ..........

Email for parent / guardian: ..........

Signature of parent / guardian: ..........

Please allow 28 days for delivery. Offer is only available while stocks last. We reserve the right to change the terms of this offer at any time and we offer a 14 day money back guarantee. This does not affect your statutory rights. Offers apply to UK only.

☐ We may occasionally wish to send you information about other Egmont children's books.
If you would rather we didn't, please tick this box.

**Ref: LIM 001**

cut along the dotted line and return this whole page